THE ADVENTURES OF THOMAS

No Joke for James *and* Diesel Does it Again

Based on the Railway Series by the Rev. W. Awdry

NO JOKE FOR JAMES

James is a mixed traffic engine. He can pull both trucks and coaches. He is proud of his smart red paint and so is his driver.

"Everyone says you brighten up their day, James."

One morning, James whistled loudly at the other engines. "Look at me. I am the smartest most useful engine on the line."

"Rubbish," replied Thomas. "We're all useful. The Fat Controller says so and he's Sir Topham Hatt, head of the whole railway."

"You know what James?" added Percy.

"What?" replied James.

"You're getting all puffed up!"

James huffed away.

Later he was still boasting. "I'm the pride of the line."

"I saw you pulling trucks today. You're only a goods engine!" snorted Gordon.

James was furious. "I pull coaches too!"

"Not as much as I do," grunted Gordon.

"But the Fat Controller has plans for me."

James was making this up but Gordon believed him.

"What plans?"

"Er—wait and see."

"Oh dear," thought James. "Now what'll I do?"

Thomas was shunting shining new coaches.

"Good morning, James."

"Are those coaches for me?" asked James hopefully.

"No. These are for Gordon's express. I'll fetch your trucks next."

But James was going to play a trick on the other engines.

"Actually Thomas, I'm taking the coaches. The Fat Controller asked me to tell you."

"What about the trucks?"

"Er—give them to Gordon."

"Come on, Thomas," said his driver, "orders are orders."

So when James's driver returned, James was coupled to the coaches and he puffed away.

Thomas returned with the trucks. A few minutes later Gordon arrived.

"Where's the express?"

Thomas told him about James. "And so here are your trucks."

Gordon was very cross and so was his driver.

"Wait till the Fat Controller hears about this!"

Meanwhile, James was enjoying himself enormously.

"What a clever plan, what a clever plan," he chuffed. Then he saw the Fat Controller.

"Some jokes are funny, but not this one James. You have caused confusion."

"Yes, Sir," said James.

"You will stay in your shed until you are wanted."

The other engines teased James.

"I wonder who'll be pulling the express today?" said Gordon.

"I expect it'll be you," replied Henry. "James is stuck in the shed for being silly!"

James felt sad.

Next morning, he went back to work.

"Hello," whistled Thomas. "Good to see you out and about again."

"I'm sorry I tricked you," said James. "Are these my trucks?"

"Yes," replied Thomas kindly. "They are pleased to have you back."

James puffed into the harbour with his goods train of trucks. He bustled about all day, pushing and pulling them into place.

"Time to go home now, James," said his driver at last. "No trucks or passengers, just we two."

But his driver was wrong.

"Excuse me," called a man. "I have a meeting with Sir Topham Hatt and I mustn't be late. May I ride back with you?"

"Of course," replied James's driver. Then he whispered to James, "This gentleman is a railway inspector."

James was most impressed. He steamed along the line as smoothly and quickly as he could.

The Fat Controller was waiting and the railway inspector greeted him warmly.

"This clever engine gave me a splendid ride. You must be proud of him."

"Yes indeed. James, once again you are a Really Useful Engine."

DIESEL DOES IT AGAIN

Duck and Percy enjoy their work at the harbour, pulling and pushing trucks full of cargo to and from the quay.

But one morning, the engines were exhausted. The harbour was busier than ever. The Fat Controller promised that another engine would be found to help them.

"It's about time," said Percy.

"I ache so much I can hardly get my wheels to move," agreed Duck.

They waited for the engine to arrive.

It came as a shock when he did.

"Good morning," squirmed Diesel in his oily voice.

The two engines had not worked with Diesel for a long time.

"What are you doing here?" gasped Duck.

"Your worthy Fat . . . Sir Topham Hatt sent me. I hope you are pleased to see me. I am to shunt some dreadfully tiresome trucks."

"Shunt where?" said Percy suspiciously.

"Where? Why from here to there . . . " purred Diesel, " . . . and then again from there to here. Easy, isn't it?"

With that, Diesel, as if to make himself quite clear, bumped some trucks hard.

"Ooooooh!" screamed the trucks.

"Grrrrh," growled Diesel.

Percy and Duck were horrified. They did not trust Diesel at all. They refused to work and would not leave their shed.

The Fat Controller was enjoying his tea and iced bun when the telephone rang.

"So, there's trouble in the harbour yard? I'll be there right away!"

Diesel was working loudly and alone.

Cargo lay on the quay. Ships and passengers were delayed. Everyone was complaining about the Fat Controller's railway.

Percy and Duck were sulking in their shed.

"What's all this?" demanded the Fat Controller.

"Er, we're on strike, Sir," said Percy.

"Yes," added Duck. "Beg pardon, Sir, but we won't work with Diesel, Sir."

Then, in a quiet hurt voice, he added, "You said you sent him packing, Sir."

"I have to give Diesel a second chance. I am trying to help you by bringing Diesel here. Now you must help me. He was the only engine available."

Percy and Duck went sadly back to work.

Next morning, things were no better. Diesel's driver had not put his brakes on properly and Diesel started to move.

He went bump, straight into Percy!

Percy had an awful fright.

"Wake up there, Percy," scowled Diesel. "You have work to do."

He didn't even say he was sorry to Percy.

Later, Diesel bumped the trucks so hard that the loads went everywhere.

"What will the Fat Controller say?" gasped Percy.

"He won't like it," said Duck.

"So who's going to tell him, I wonder?" said Diesel. "Two little goody-goody tell-tales like you, I suppose."

Percy and Duck did not want to be tell-tales, so they said nothing. Diesel, thinking he could get away with his bad behaviour, was ruder than ever.

Next day he was shunting trucks full of china clay. He banged the trucks hard into the buffers, but the buffers weren't secure.

The silly trucks were sunk.

Soon the Fat Controller heard the news. The trucks were hoisted safely from the sea, but the clay was lost.

The Fat Controller spoke severely to Diesel.

"Things worked much better here before you arrived. I shall not be inviting you back."

"Now Duck and Percy, I hope you won't mind having to handle the work by yourselves again."

"Oh no, Sir. Yes please, Sir," replied the engines.

Whistling cheerfully, they puffed back to work while Diesel sulked slowly away.

First published in Great Britain 1995
by Mammoth, an imprint of
Reed Children's Books
Michelin House, 81 Fulham Road, London SW3 6RB
AUCKLAND - MELBOURNE - SINGAPORE - TORONTO

Reprinted 1995

ISBN 0-7497-2018-2

Printed in Great Britain by Cambus Litho